KU-034-334

THIS BOOK BELONGS TO

_____

I am a reader and I celebrated World Book Day 2024

with this gift from my local bookseller and

Hodder Children's Books.

WORLD BOOK DAY®

World Book Day's mission is to offer every child and young person the opportunity to read and love books by giving you the chance to have a book of your own.

To find out more, and for fun activities including the monthly World Book Day Book Club, video stories and book recommendations, visit worldbookday.com

World Book Day is a charity sponsored by National Book Tokens.

THE AMAZING EDIE ECKHART

THE FRIEND MISSION

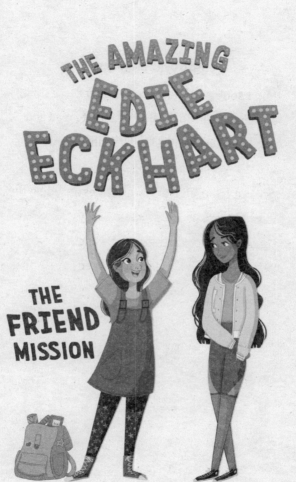

Also by Rosie Jones

The Amazing Edie Eckhart

The Amazing Edie Eckhart: The Big Trip

THE AMAZING EDIE ECKHART

THE FRIEND MISSION

ROSIE JONES

ILLUSTRATED BY NATALIE SMILLIE AND LEO TRINIDAD

HODDER

HODDER CHILDREN'S BOOKS

First published in Great Britain in 2024 by Hodder & Stoughton

1 3 5 7 9 10 8 6 4 2

A CIP catalogue record for this book
is available from the British Library.

Paperback ISBN: 978 1 444 97458 4

Export ISBN: 978 1 444 97459 1

Typeset in Duper OT by Jouve (UK), Milton Keynes
Printed and bound in Great Britain by Clays Ltd, Elcograf S.p.A.

The paper and board used in this book
are made from wood from responsible sources.

MIX
Paper from
responsible sources
FSC® C104740

Hodder Children's Books
An imprint of
Hachette Children's Group
Part of Hodder & Stoughton Limited
Carmelite House
50 Victoria Embankment
London EC4Y 0DZ

An Hachette UK Company
www.hachette.co.uk

www.hachettechildrens.co.uk

This book is dedicated to YOU. Whether you are a fan of Edie already, or whether this is your first step into the world of *The Amazing Edie Eckhart*, I hope you enjoy this little book for you!

2nd September – 8.02am

'Oscar, stop yanking every tree branch we walk under!' I tap my best friend on the shoulder. We are walking to school and it's the first day back after the summer holidays. I am sooooo excited. This year we'll be in Year 8, which feels properly grown up. We are no longer the new kids at school, woo hoo!

Oscar is less thrilled about returning to class though, in fact, he's not happy *at all*. Every tree he walks past, he holds down a branch and flings it back on to itself, scowling all the while.

'If you're not careful, you'll hit your own face with one,' I warn him. 'And I'll have no choice but to laugh, because that would be pretty funny.'

He scowls at me even more. When he's moody, he doesn't like when I tease him.

'I just don't understand why we still need to go to school,' Oscar mumbles. 'I feel like I know everything already.'

Oscar is clever, but he's not *that* clever.

'Osc, do you know what trigonometry is?' I ask him.

'What's that?'

'Exactly, come on.'

We enter the school gates, arm in arm. When I walk anywhere with any of my friends, I link arms with them, because it helps me walk. I have a disability called cerebral palsy, which means that I wobble when I walk, and I fall over a lot. I speak slowly too, and sometimes, (especially when I'm tired) some people find it a bit difficult to understand what I am saying.

'Meet you at lunch, Edie?' Oscar asks me, still scowling under his hat. Even though it's not really cold, Oscar is still wearing his favourite orange beanie.

'Yes, but only if you cheer up!' I playfully prod Oscar in the ribs, and he smiles for the first time this morning.

'Fine!' Oscar reluctantly agrees, and waves me goodbye, heading to his tutor room.

I turn and walk into my classroom.

'Edie!' I look up and I see my old tutor, Mrs Adler.

'Miss, you're back!' I can't stop smiling. Mrs Adler is probably my favourite teacher *ever*. She was my tutor for Year 7, but she left school last Christmas to give birth to two baby girls and has been on parental leave since then.

I really want to hug her but that would be a bit weird, wouldn't it? So I settle for a giddy wave. I hope she's going to bring in the babies to meet us all soon. I love babies. They are super cute and squishy!

I realise that I am one of the last people to sit down, so I rush to my seat, right near the front.

Who's that, then?

Standing next to Mrs Adler is a very tall, beautiful girl, with wavy black hair. She looks shy. I smile at her to be friendly, but I don't think she sees me.

'Good morning, everyone. Settle down now, thank you. It's lovely to be back with you all, and especially to introduce someone new to the class. This is Mia,' Mrs Adler explains. 'She's a new joiner to our school and she is from America. I'd like you all to help make Mia feel at home here.'

America! I don't think I've ever met somebody from America before, this is thrilling. I've seen loads of American people on television but never in real life. I already have a million questions for her. I've heard that the pizza slices are massive over there.

'Why don't you tell the class something about where you're from, Mia,' Mrs Adler encourages, facing her.

Mia shrugs and looks down at her feet. 'Hi, erm . . . so my name's Mia, and . . . erm, I'm from a city called San Francisco.'

Mia talks a bit funny. Has she got cerebral palsy too? I look at her legs. She doesn't *seem* to be wobbly.

Mrs Adler turns to Mia, and asks, 'Would you prefer to explain your hearing aids to the class, or would you like me to do it?'

She points at Mrs Adler, and then she stares at the floor, looking embarrassed.

'Mia has a hearing impairment, which is why she is wearing hearing aids. She uses American Sign Language and lip-reads too, so we all need to remember to face Mia when we are talking to her. Can we now give Mia a big, loud, Year Eight "hello"?' says Mrs Adler.

'Hello!' the class yells, and Mia goes bright red.

Mrs Adler points at the empty chair next to me. 'Edie, is it OK if Mia sits next to you?'

I nod enthusiastically. 'Of course it is, miss!'

Mia quickly sits down and fidgets her hands nervously.

I remember how scary it felt when I started at secondary school last year, but at least I knew Oscar from my old school. I can't even imagine how scary it would be to start a new school in a whole new country. No wonder Mia keeps looking down and away, she must be terrified.

'Hello, Mia. My name is Edie Eckhart,' I face her directly, to make sure that she understands what I'm saying.

But Mia mustn't be able to hear me because she doesn't look at me.

'Anyway,' Mrs Adler claps her hands, 'now we're back and settled, welcome to Year Eight!'

12.34pm

'What have you got in your sandwich, Edie?' Oscar asks
me at lunchtime. We sometimes like to swap
sandwiches, so we get half of each other's. It's generally
a win-win situation.

'Cheese and Marmite,' I say proudly.

'Cheese and *Marmite*?' Oscar shivers in disgust.
'Since when do you like Marmite?'

'Flora made it for me over the summer and it is
seriously delicious.'

Oscar rolls his eyes. 'Oh, well, if *Flora* likes it.'

'Oi!' I snort indignantly, poking Oscar in the side. 'You
love Flora. Sometimes I think you love Flora more than
you love me, even though we both know that's
impossible.'

Flora is my brilliant girlfriend. We met nearly a year
ago when we were working on the same play together,
A Christmas Carol by Charles Dickens. I played
Scrooge, and Flora did the set design,

because she is an amazing artist.

'Speaking about me, are you?' I look up and I see Flora walking towards us. I can't help but smile a mile wide. She sits down next to me and without saying another word she leans over and takes a bite of my sandwich. I giggle.

'Mmm, delicious,' agrees Flora.

Oscar throws his hands up in despair. 'You two are beyond weird!'

Flora

'Thank you, Oscar. Proud to be weird.' Flora squeezes my hand. 'How was the first morning of being in Year Eight?'

'Good, I think,' I tell her. 'We have a new girl in our class. She's called Mia and she's moved here from America.'

'No way,' Oscar laughs. 'That is such a funny coincidence, because we have a new *boy*, Benjamin, in our class who is also from America.'

'Oscar, that can't be a coincidence!

They're probably brother and sister. Oooh, or maybe even twins like Mrs Adler's babies.'

'Probably twins if they're in the same year,' Flora agrees.

'Oh, there they are!' I point over to the other side of the courtyard, where I can see Mia standing with a boy who's just as tall as she is and has floppy dark hair. 'They are *definitely* twins. They look so alike!'

'Why aren't they talking?' Oscar asks.

'They're signing, Oscar – they're communicating with their hands and facial expressions, because Mia has a hearing impairment,' I explain.

'I've always wanted to learn sign language, that's cool,' Flora says. 'I wonder what they are saying. Did you talk to her in class?'

I shake my head. 'I

don't think she wanted to talk very much,' I admit. 'She seemed really shy.'

'Benjamin didn't really say much in my tutor group either. He just kind of sat at the back on his own with a sketchbook,' says Oscar.

I look over at the twins, and I feel sad. I want them to feel like they can talk to us, instead of just hanging out with each other. I feel like Year 8 hasn't been that welcoming so far for them. Maybe I should do something.

'Don't, Edie.' Oscar warns me.

'What? I didn't even say anything!'

'I've known you for nine years, and I know when you're planning something. You're a meddler, you are.'

Flora laughs. 'I hate to say it but he's got a point, Edie. You do like getting involved with things. In a great way though,' she adds at the end, just in case I'm offended.

But I'm not. I just want to help if I can. 'Cos that's who I am. Edie Eckhart – and I am on a mission!

Me, my mum and dad, and my little brother, Louie, are sitting round the dinner table, eating, laughing and talking. This is one of my favourite parts of the day because we all take it in turns to update each other on what we've been up to.

My dad is a paediatrician – that's a doctor who looks after children – so his days are always a little bit interesting, and a little bit gross. Today he had to look after a boy who had broken his leg so badly, part of his bone was bursting out of the skin.

'Not whilst we're eating, love,' Mum warns him, and Dad shrugs his shoulders like *What did I say?*

'Aw, why not? I find it so cool,' Louie gleefully yells, adding, 'I love blood.'

'Well, you're your father's son, all right,' says Mum before turning to me and asking, 'how was your first day back, Edie?'

I nod, quickly swallowing the big piece of lasagne I

just popped in my mouth. 'Really good. Mrs Adler's back from having her babies, and we've got a new girl in our tutor group. She's from America.'

'Please can I go to America, Mummy? I'm definitely big enough now, right?' Louie asks her, widening his big eyes, and looking so cute. Even though he's in Year 1, I still think of him as my cute, teeny tiny baby brother.

'Not on your own, and not unless you finish all of your dinner.' Mum ruffles his hair and Louie giggles. 'That's great, Edie, I know you really liked Mrs Adler before. Did you get the chance to talk to the new girl?'

'Not really, she seems quite shy. She has a twin brother, who's in Oscar's class, so at lunch they just hung out with each other. She's Deaf, too.'

I immediately feel a bit weird mentioning Mia's hearing impairment. I don't know if this was a relevant bit of information to share. I would hate it if somebody was describing me and they just said, 'Edie has cerebral palsy,' and that was it, because even though I do, I think my disability is, like, the least interesting part of me.

Maybe I mentioned her disability because that is literally all I know about her. Tomorrow I am going to try and talk to Mia properly.

I think back to when I was first getting to know Flora. Sometimes I used to think she was really, really moody, but actually she was just shy. Maybe with a bit of encouraging, Mia might open up and want to be my friend, like Flora did.

If I make Mia realise that there's nothing to be scared of at our school, and that actually we are just as friendly as her American friends, she might relax, and I could properly get to know her.

'Starting a new school can seem really scary, poppet. Especially if you come from a whole new country,' Dad comments, as if he can read my mind. 'You're thinking about what you can do to help her settle in, aren't you?'

I nod distractedly, because I am still thinking about a plan to get Mia to talk to me. 'I just would like to think that if I started a new school, somebody would try to be my friend. I know I can be that person for Mia.'

Mum kisses my forehead. 'Edie, you might just be the kindest person I know.'

I smile at her, mission accepted!

3rd September – 8.12am

'Pizza?' Oscar asks me, with a really surprised look on his face.

'Yep.' I nod, glad that he immediately understands my plan. 'I'm going to ask her what her favourite pizza topping is. She's from America and it's a fact that everybody from America *loves* pizza.'

'Everybody? What about people who are lactose intolerant?'

I can tell that Oscar is trying to be clever, so immediately I answer, 'Vegan cheese.'

Oscar laughs. 'Fine, but if her favourite pizza topping is pineapple, we are *not* going to be her friend.'

'Oscar, this is not about judging a person on their favourite pizza topping! I am just using the question to get her to talk with me. And you should talk to Benjamin too. Invite him to sit with us at lunch.'

'Fine, but if he likes pineapple on pizza, he's out.'

'Remember, I quite like pineapple on a pizza,' I say, half serious, half to wind him up.

'First pineapple on pizza, now Marmite. Edie, do I even know you any more?' Oscar exclaims.

'Course you do,' I laugh. 'But that's the great thing about friendship, isn't it? Finding out new stuff about each other all of the time. It keeps it interesting.'

'If you say so. I'd be happy with jam sandwiches and pepperoni pizza for the rest of my life.' Oscar closes his eyes and pats his stomach contentedly.

I roll my eyes at my best friend, and head into my tutor group.

Today I am one of the first people to get there. 'Morning, miss,' I say to Mrs Adler, who is sat at her desk, typing something on her laptop.

'Morning, Edie. How was your first day of Year Eight yesterday?' she asks, stopping typing to look up at me.

'Really good, thank you. I'm so happy you're back, miss. It really wasn't the same without you here. How was your day?'

'Oh, thank you very much, Edie, how kind of you to say. I am so happy to be back and my day was equally as good.' Mrs Adler yawns, quickly covering her mouth with her hand. 'Oh, sorry. I tell you what is *not* good. The twins waking us up at one a.m., and two a.m., and four a.m., et cetera.'

Nearly *every* hour?! Wow, babies really are demanding. I thought it was bad when Louie woke me up at five because he had a bad dream. But that's only happened, like, three times ever. I seriously don't think I could get out of bed the next morning if that was me.

'Thank you for encouraging Mia to sit next to you yesterday.'

'No problem, miss. Starting a new school is scary. And it must be even more scary in a different country.'

'I had to start at a new school when I was in Year Nine, and I really disliked it at first,' confides Mrs Adler. 'But it got so much better once I started making new friends. I'm still friends with them, even after all these many, many years.'

'Miss?' I pause because I haven't really thought through what I'm asking. 'Is there anything the school does for new students . . . like an induction, or like a tour or anything?'

Mrs Adler thinks about this before answering. 'New students usually get a tour of the school before they start – but maybe Mia and Benjamin didn't get that because they were still in America. I'm afraid I don't know, Edie—'

Mrs Adler is cut off when the classroom door bursts open, and a long line of kids pile through, including Mia. She raises her eyebrows at me, as if to say hello, and sits down in her chair.

'Do you like pizza?' I ask, facing her, to make sure that she can read my lips.

'What?' she replies, looking really confused.

Oh no, maybe I should've started with a simple 'hello' or a 'how are you' like normal people do, instead of going right into the pizza chat.

'Piz-za . . .' I repeat, trying to pretend to cut up slices of a pizza and eat it.

'Look, Edie, I know why the teacher sat us next to each other,' Mia says, pointedly staring away from me. 'It's because you have something wrong with you and I do too, am I right? But just because we're both disabled, it doesn't mean we'll get on. Maybe we shouldn't be friends *because* we both have disabilities,' Mia blurts out, cold and blunt.

I feel like I've been hit in the face with a tree branch. No one has ever said anything like that to me before. I don't even know where to start with that, but one thing's for sure: I wasn't trying to get to know Mia just because she was disabled, I wanted her to feel comfortable and welcome because she's new and being new is scary, and she doesn't know anybody yet.

Part of me wants to run away and cry, but I decide to be strong, and so I say, 'I don't think Mrs Adler sat you next to me because we are both disabled. I think she sat you here because it's at the front so you can lip-read her, and she knows that I like making friends. And I don't have anything *wrong* with me. I have cerebral palsy, and I'm proud to have it. There's nothing wrong with that.'

Mia's cheeks are glowing red. And when I look closer, I see that she now looks really sad. Oh no. I didn't mean to make her sad. 'Sorry. I—'

'Right, hello, happy Tuesday, one and all!' Mrs Adler sings, in her usually cheery tone, then ploughs straight into taking the register. Nobody would know that she's been up half the night with her babies.

And as soon as the bell rings for first lesson, Mia sprints away, and I don't see her for the rest of the morning.

12.15pm

'Benjamin's joining us for lunch,' Oscar informs me as we sit outside in the courtyard. It is a really sunny day today, so Oscar lays his sweater down and sits on the grass. 'He's actually really great. Funny too. I haven't asked him what his favourite pizza topping is yet though, so that could all change. Is Mia coming?' Oscar peels open his tin foil package to reveal what sandwich his mum has made him. 'Yes! Jam. Get in.'

I shrug. 'I don't know, maybe not. I didn't get a chance to ask her. It all kind of went a bit wrong with the pizza thing,' I admit, not sure how to explain the rest of it yet.

'Oh, don't take it so hard, Edie. Not every plan works straight away. She might come over with her brother anyway,' Oscar says kindly.

I open my sandwich, keen to change the subject all of a sudden. 'Ham . . . would sir be open to a swap?' I say, putting on a posh voice.

'Hmmm, a jam for a ham? I could do a jam for a ham, indeed. Quite the deal, my fellow,' Oscar answers in an equally posh voice, which makes me giggle more than I have all morning. We shake hands, like two business people settling on a deal.

'Hi there.' We both look up to see Benjamin is standing right next to us, smiling. Slightly behind him is Mia. 'Do you mind if we join you? This is my sister Mia.'

Benjamin speaks to us but uses sign language too. I guess that is for Mia, so she understands what he's saying to us. I think that is so cool. I find it really hard to do two things at once, like patting your head and rubbing your tummy. I always get confused and end up patting my head AND my tummy. Oscar does that too.

'HELLO – MIA. PLEASED – TO – MEET – YOU. I'M OSCAR!' Oscar shouts, enunciating every word.

I want to shout at him and tell him that just because she is Deaf, it doesn't mean she's stupid.

'Hi, Oscar,' Mia says quietly.

'Sit down, sit down, both of you. We're just swapping sandwiches. Jam for a ham.' Oscar says, dramatically displaying our sandwiches like they're priceless vases.

Benjamin laughs, and I can see he has a big, friendly smile. 'Jam . . . I need to get used to saying that. We call it jelly.'

'Really?' Oscar asks. 'But if jam is jelly, what is *jelly* jelly, then?' He wobbles his hands like he's trying to hold a bowl full of it.

'Jell-O,' Mia responds, emphasising the 'O'.

Oscar shakes his head hard. 'Whoa, that is so funny. At least now I know what to do if I'm ever in America and I want to order jelly, oops, sorry, Jell-O.'

'There are just a few differences between British and American, but did you know British Sign Language is a whole different language to American Sign Language? There are a few words that are similar, but most are totally different. As soon as our parents told us we were moving here for good, Mia and me have been learning BSL too,' Benjamin tells us.

I feel even more impressed than I was already. I had no idea that there were different types of sign language. How cool is that?

Then Flora rushes over. I don't think I have ever seen her look so stressed. Her usually straight and unmoving dark hair is flying all over the place, in the same rhythm as her quick, direct walking. I immediately feel sad. I don't like it when Flora is upset because I care about her so much. How can she feel this way on the second day of term?

'Miss Jamison hates me,' she says, with her bottom lip curling over. She looks exactly like a sad emoji. Cute but undeniably sad. I immediately give her my biggest hug.

Miss Jamison is the art teacher. She's pretty young for a teacher, and beautiful, and she always wears really bright, fun dresses. She also has her nose pierced, which is seriously cool. I can't imagine why Flora thinks she hates her, given that Flora is an incredible artist.

'She doesn't, Flora,' Oscar reassures her. 'You're, like, her favourite student – if she had favourites. And I don't think she has the ability to hate *anybody*, she's that nice.'

'You would say that, Oscar,' groans Flora. 'You have a crush on her.'

I can't help but laugh because Flora is so right. Oscar *totally* has a crush on Miss Jamison. Whenever she walks past us in the corridor and says hello, he goes bright red and loses the ability to speak.

'No I don't, I just think she's really nice, and funny, and beautiful and clever, and . . .' Oscar pauses mid-thought. 'Oh no, OK, I might have a crush on her! But this isn't about me, this is about *Flora*. Why do you think she hates you?'

'Which she doesn't,' I add quickly, to make sure Flora knows that this isn't true.

'She really does.' Flora takes a sketchbook out of her backpack. 'She said my piece "lacked heart".'

I see Benjamin and Mia share a secret glance. I wonder if they've met Miss Jamison yet.

'I had my first art lesson with Miss Jamison today. She seemed nice, but that sounds real harsh – and hi, I'm Benjamin,' he adds.

We had all been so wrapped up in making sure that Flora was OK, we forgot to introduce her to Mia and Benjamin.

'And this is Mia, Benjamin's sister,' I tell Flora. 'We're in the same tutor group.'

'Oh hi, Mia and Benjamin, good to meet you. Sorry for going off on one,' Flora says with the start of a smile. Mia nods back.

'Whoa, they get really strict in Year Nine!' Oscar shakes his head.

'Can we see it?' I ask Flora, and suddenly she looks a bit nervous.

'Well, yes, but it was meant to be an early Christmas present to you, Edie. So don't be disappointed if you think it's rubbish too.'

Flora opens up her sketchbook and reveals a painting of . . . It's *me*.

'Flora, I love it,' I say, because I really do.

'Miss Jamison doesn't, clearly.'

'Well, I do too,' Benjamin suddenly chips in. 'That picture is amazing, I mean it.'

Benjamin opens up his rucksack and pulls out a packet of children's colouring pencils.

'OK, this might sound kiddy, but I do a lot of my artwork with these pencils. I love how I can make the colours *pop* by dabbing them in some water. Can I show you?'

Flora nods, and hands him her sketchbook. He dips the tip of a pencil in his water bottle, then begins to colour in the red dollop of sauce on the hot dog. It's like it literally becomes ketchup – I can almost taste it! He uses his little finger to smudge and blend with oranges and yellows on the roll too.

We all watch him silently, amazed at how the picture comes to life before our eyes.

'That's awesome, Benjamin. Do you do portraits too?' asks Flora.

He shakes his head and pulls out a sketchbook from his bag before continuing to sign for his sister as he speaks. 'I don't really draw people. I like to draw buildings and structures. I want to be an architect. Here's one I did of back home.'

'Whoa, that is so cool. Is that the Golden Gate Bridge?' I say, looking at the epic and complicated brilliant red bridge in Benjamin's sketchbook.

'Yup, that's the one. We could see it from the roof of our apartment.'

'We don't really have bridges like that in Bridlington. All we have is the Humber Bridge in Hull, and that one's just boring grey.' Oscar laughs.

'Do you draw too?' I ask Mia. I am aware that she hasn't spoken for ages, and I don't want her to feel left out. Regardless of how our last conversation went, I want her to feel a part of this one.

Mia shakes her head.

'Mia is the athlete of our family,' Benjamin explains, looking very proud of his twin sister.

'Wow, what sports?' Oscar asks enthusiastically. 'Me and Flora play football. Or I think you know it as soccer!'

Oh no, I hope she isn't a football fan too. I spend too many Saturdays as it is in the freezing cold, watching my best friend and my girlfriend play football. Not sure I can handle another football fan in our group! Secretly I do love it, but mainly just for the food at half-time.

'Running. Long distance especially. Not so much team sports,' replies Mia.

'Well, if you're ever wanting to give football a go, we always could do with an extra player on our team,' Flora offers.

'Oi! Why don't you ever ask me to join your team,

Flora. Is it because I'm disabled?' I pipe up with a cheeky expression on my face.

Flora and Oscar look at me, then each other, and roll their eyes.

'No, Edie,' she replies, complementing my performance perfectly. 'It's because you have zero interest in the game and you only come to football matches for the snacks.'

We all laugh, and Flora squeezes my hand and kisses the knuckles. They're both used to me making jokes about my disability, and they know that I like it when they make fun of it back to me. I don't find it a thing to be upset or ashamed about. It is just a part of me.

I glance over to Mia and I can't help feeling disappointed to see she is looking embarrassed again. Disappointed but then also bad for feeling disappointed. She quickly signs something to Benjamin. I don't understand what she is saying, but she seems to be pointing away from us.

'Hey, folks. Mia just remembered that she left her water bottle in the classroom so we're gonna head off.

We'll see you around,' says Benjamin.

Flora and Oscar look surprised, and then Flora goes to hand Benjamin back his pack of colouring pencils.

'Keep them. And good luck with the piece.'

Mia and Benjamin quickly gather up their things and walk swiftly back into school.

'She hates me,' I admit to my friends, looking away because I don't want Flora and Oscar to know how upset I am.

'No she doesn't, she's just shy,' Oscar tells me.

I shake my head at him hard. 'This morning she told me that "just because we're both disabled, it doesn't mean we'll get on", and that "there's something wrong with both of us". I wasn't trying to get to know her because she's disabled, I was trying to get to know her because she's new and she doesn't know anyone!'

'Well, that's not a nice thing to say. Maybe I hate *her*.' Flora scowls. Sometimes she reminds me of a fierce lioness. When somebody she cares about is sad, she goes into mega protective mode and will fight anybody who has upset them.

'Don't hate her, Flora, just because she hates me. I'm not sure that helps anyone. I still want Mia to have friends. Even if that friend isn't me. Hey, why don't we invite her and Benjamin to the beach at the weekend?'

'Are you sure, Edie? Saturday is meant to be just the three of us, hanging out,' Flora asks me, looking unsure.

I nod with determination. I feel like my mission has moved into Plan B. 'Oscar, you ask Benjamin in tutor group tomorrow if they're both free on Saturday. That's that.'

Oscar nods, and then after a few seconds, asks, 'Erm, Edie, who made you the boss, when you're the smallest?'

'I might be the smallest, but I am the loudest, so what I say goes!' I shout.

We all laugh, and I tuck into my jam – I mean *jelly* – sandwich. Delicious.

7th September — 11.25am

The rest of the week zoomed by and on Saturday Oscar, Flora and I get to the beach before Mia and Benjamin. It's a beautiful sunny day and the waves are sparkling like diamonds. I don't know why, but I feel really nervous.

'What if they don't show up?' I ask them both.

'If they don't show up, they don't show up. And we have a lovely day, just the three of us, like we planned to do anyway,' Flora reassures me.

'And it IS only,' Oscar checks his phone, '11.25, and we said we would meet them at 11.30. That's a whole five minutes away.'

I think I am just nervous because for the entire week Mia has barely said two words to me. She says hello in the morning, but only if I say hello to her first. And then we just spend the rest of the time sitting next to each other, in silence.

'Hey, early birds!' we look behind, and we see Benjamin and Mia walking down the ramp towards us on the beach. Benjamin is waving at us, and Mia is walking a few steps behind him.

'I brought towels and a football, so I have literally everything we need,' Oscar declares.

'Are we going in the sea?' Benjamin asks, suddenly looking hesitant. 'It might be sunny but this isn't exactly California weather.'

I laugh and shake my head. 'You can, but I'm definitely not. Sometimes if I am feeling brave enough, I will pop my feet in but there's no CHANCE that I'm getting right in. It's Freezing with a capital F!'

Everybody laughs, and I notice Mia smiles. Maybe she does like me, just a little bit.

'Oh!' Flora jumps towards her bag quickly, as if she's just remembered something, and pulls out her sketchbook and Benjamin's packet of colouring pencils. 'Before I forget, thank you for lending me these . . . and here we are!'

Flora opens her sketchbook to the page with my portrait with the hot dog. It looks A-mazing.

'Miss Jamison said that I "captured the subject perfectly" and it has lots of heart. So thank you, those colouring pencils saved me,' Flora says warmly.

Benjamin takes back the packet and smiles. 'Glad I could help. Every artist has to show their critics sometimes, you know? Are you going to draw anything today?'

Flora shrugs. 'Probably. I haven't decided yet. But first I think we're going to play football. Do you fancy it?'

Benjamin shakes his head. 'No, no, I am more of a sitter downer, rather than a kicky baller guy.'

I laugh. 'Me too.'

'Mia, d'you want to play?' Oscar asks, and she gives him a thumbs-up.

The three of them run to a wide stretch of flat sand with two beach towels to use as goal posts. Benjamin sits next to me.

'She likes you, you know.'

I must look confused because Benjamin repeats it.

'Mia really likes you, Edie. She came home last night and told me that you're the only person who remembers to face her when they are talking every single time. So thank you.'

I don't really know what to say. It doesn't take much to remember to face somebody. It's like Oscar remembering to link arms with me when we walk long distances. 'Don't thank me, that's just common sense.' I bat my hand away and take a deep breath. 'Benjamin, I thought Mia hated me.'

He smiles to himself and lowers his voice. 'I'm her twin brother and sometimes I'm convinced that she hates *me*.'

I laugh and watch the three of them playing football in the distance. Mia runs like lightning and before Oscar can get back in goal, she's passed it to Flora, who boots it through the goalposts. Even though Mia has been a little bit mean to me this week, I still find myself hoping we can be friends.

'This whole thing has been really hard for my sis: moving to another country and meeting new people. I'm a lot more sociable than she is but I've still found it hard. And being hearing makes it easier for me also,' Benjamin tells me.

'Did Mia leave a lot of friends back in America?' I ask.

I try to imagine leaving Oscar, Flora and all my other friends to go to a new school *and* in a new country. That sounds *terrible*. I would definitely find that hard too.

But Benjamin shakes his head. 'Not really,' he says, playing with the sand under his fingers and looking upset. 'A lot of people picked on her, especially when she started wearing hearing aids. I tried to stick up for her and fight the bullies, but that just made it worse.'

I am so surprised. I look over to Mia. Now it's her turn in goal, blocking the penalty strikes being shot at her by Oscar and Flora. She is laughing and smiling with her whole face. It makes me so angry to think that anybody could make fun of her for something she has no choice about having.

At the same time, I feel lucky that I have never been bullied. Sometimes, in primary school, other kids would call me names, but I never let it bother me. I always had

Oscar by my side, and when he's around I don't care what other people think about me.

Before Benjamin continues any further, I say what I've just realised. 'Mia's frightened that if she becomes friends with me, it'll attract attention, and the bullying will start again. Even though nothing's suggested that's going to happen here.'

Benjamin looks so relieved that I get it. 'Well, I know that, but try telling her. She's so stubborn!'

I can't help but laugh because that's what people describe me as, too.

'DRINK BREAK!' Oscar calls out, and I see the three of them jogging back to where me and Benjamin are sitting. 'Look, we already know the British sign for football,' he says excitedly.

In unison, the three of them move each forefinger around, and it looks like legs running up and down.

'Who wants something from the shop? Cokes all round? I'll get them. Mia, what's the British sign for drink?'

Mia shows him and he copies it, looking proud of

himself. We all nod for Cokes, and Oscar jogs off the beach and to the shop nearby.

Mia flops down on the sand beside me and leans back with her eyes closed and the sun on her face. She looks the happiest I've seen her yet.

Benjamin suddenly gets up and brushes the sand from his jeans. 'What's that in the distance?' he asks, pointing towards the harbour. 'I'm gonna go take a closer look so I can draw it.'

'That's Bridlington Harbour,' Flora tells him. 'I'll walk with you.'

They both grab their pencils and sketchbooks and head off. Suddenly it's just me and Mia, sitting together on the beach.

'You're pretty great at football,' I say, facing her, and signing 'football', because it is the only sign I know. That, and 'drink'.

'Thank you.' Mia smiles slightly then adds, 'It was more fun than I thought it would be.'

We sit in silence for what feels like forever, but it must only be a few seconds.

'I am so sorry if I ever made you feel uncomfortable, talking about my disability in the way that I do,' I say, hoping that she will accept my apology. 'Sometimes I am so used to it, I forget that other people find it a bit strange.'

'I don't find it strange, I find it wonderful,' Mia says, her eyes filling with tears. 'I wish I could be as confident as you.'

'I'm not like this all the time,' I assure her. 'Sometimes, especially if I'm tired, or I keep falling over, I don't feel confident at all. And I think that things would be easier if I didn't have cerebral palsy and I was just like everybody else.'

I've never admitted that to anybody else before. Not to Oscar or my mum. Not even to Flora. But I instinctively feel like Mia might understand how I feel when I have a difficult day.

Mia looks at me, surprised, then asks earnestly, 'What do you do when you feel like that?'

'I talk. Sometimes to my parents, and sometimes to Oscar, or Flora, or any one of my other friends. I let them know I'm not feeling so great that day. Talking helps. Friends help. I can help.'

A tear runs down Mia's cheek and everything that's been in her head tumbles out. 'Are you sure you still want to be friends with me? I've been so mean to you ever since I got here. I was really scared of being grouped in together just because we're both different and getting bullied again, like I was in San Francisco. I didn't want to accept becoming friends with you at first because you're also disabled. But that's just the worst. I'm really so very sorry, Edie.'

I reach into my dungaree pocket, pull out a clean tissue and hand it to her. 'Please can I give you a hug?'

Mia nods as a tearful quiet smile begins to show on her face and we hug each other close.

And then afterwards, I tell her what's in my head

too. 'I totally understand you feeling like this. We are two different people, with totally different personalities: I hate running, and you love it. No idea why!'

She laughs out loud at this.

'But there is sometimes an understanding amongst disabled people,' I continue. 'I know what it feels like to be the person that everybody stares at when she walks into a room or starts talking.'

'It's rubbish,' Mia whispers, as if she is admitting a secret to me.

I nod then take a deep breath before continuing. 'But it's easier when you hang out with people who like you. I'm not saying we should be best friends forever immediately, but don't write me off just because of my disability.'

Mia has been studying my face intently the whole time I've been speaking. She takes a deep breath herself then says firmly, 'OK, deal.'

We have one more tight hug and when we break away, I see Oscar struggling down the ramp with five cans of Coke in his hands.

Mia sees him too and runs to give him a hand.

'How do you say "thank you" in sign, Mia?' Oscar asks as they join me back on the beach.

Mia touches her chin with her four fingers then takes them away whilst mouthing the words 'thank you'. Oscar copies the gesture.

'Thank you. Eh, Edie, I'm getting good at this.'

'You know, like, three signs, Osc,' I tease him, though admittedly I hardly know any myself.

'I could teach you more,' Mia offers with another shy smile. 'That might even help me practising British Sign Language too.'

'Oooh oooh, let's ask Mrs Adler first thing on Monday if you could run sign language classes at school!' I blurt out.

I immediately regret saying this. *Well done, Edie. She's just confided in you about feeling self-conscious about her disability, and now here you are, making it all about her disability.*

'Do you think people would like that?' Mia asks nervously.

'Totally, you have your first two students right here.' Oscar grins.

'Make that three!' Flora calls out as she walks towards us. 'Oscar, chuck us a Coke.'

Oscar throws one to Flora, who opens it carefully to avoid the fizz. Then he lobs one to Benjamin, who misses, and the can lands with a splat in the sand.

'Told you I'm bad at all sports,' Benjamin says, laughing.

We all laugh with him and together we sip our Cokes on the beach. I feel so happy.

9th September – 8.01am

I wait with Mia outside our classroom – we're here even earlier today than I was last week. 'Can you come in with me?' she asks.

'Of course,' I reply.

We knock on the door and wait for the always cheery no matter how tired, 'Come in!'

Mrs Adler looks up and looks thrilled to see us. 'Oh hello, you two. Did you walk to school together this morning?'

We both look at each other and nod enthusiastically.

'Oh, I am so glad to hear that you're beginning to make new friends here, Mia. I know it can be daunting at first, but we are a very friendly bunch, I promise,' says Mrs Adler.

I glance again at Mia, and she nods to tell me to say what we planned as we sat watching the waves roll in at the beach on Saturday.

'Actually, miss, that is what we wanted to talk to you about. We're friends now, but Mia found it a bit difficult settling in, didn't you?'

Mia nods vigorously and then continues our pitch. 'So we wondered if we could set up a new school policy where each tutor group nominates a class counsellor. Like someone to help new pupils settle in.'

'We just never want anybody to feel alone again.' I add.

I look over to Mia and smile at her. We practised the speech on the walk to school this morning, but that went even better than we had planned.

Mrs Adler looks at us. 'Wow, did you come up with that plan this weekend?'

We grin at our teacher and both nod at the same time.

'Well, I will have to ask the head teacher what she thinks, but personally I think it's a great idea,' Mrs Adler says. 'I've been thinking for a while that our new starters process has long been in need of an overhaul. This could be just the thing to get that going.'

Yes! Get in. I am Thrilled with a capital T!

'One more thing too,' Mia adds. 'I was wondering if I could start signing classes in British Sign Language, for anybody wanting to learn.'

'Absolutely, Mia, that is another great idea. It looks to me like Edie will be signing up immediately. And I know I'd love to have some expert tuition too!'

I grin. 'Yep, and Oscar, and Flora, and pretty much all of our friends.'

'Excellent. Consider it done. I'll work out which lunchtime this classroom is free, and Mia, I will give you free rein over the classroom for your lessons. I'll even let you use my special board pens – as Edie knows, that is an exclusive VIP privilege,' says Mrs Adler with a wink.

We laugh, and the rest of our tutor group start pouring into the classroom. We're suddenly surrounded by a sea of noise and excited early morning chatter.

'We did it!' I mouth to Mia, facing her. 'Mission successful!'

She signs 'thank you', and I am so glad I know what that means. I can't wait to learn more sign language from my new friend Mia, but for now I've got exactly what I need to say.

I shake my head with the biggest smile on my face and then sign 'thank *you*' back at her.

ROSIE JONES is a comedian, actor and writer. She has fronted her own travelogue series called *Trip Hazard* on Channel 4 and can also be seen on countless hit television shows, including *Live At The Apollo*, *The Jonathan Ross Show*, *The Last Leg* and *Casualty*, to name a few!

In her spare time, Rosie loves seeing her friends, eating sausage rolls and Scotch eggs, listening to Taylor Swift, and playing *Candy Crush*.

Have you read the first two books in the series?

The
ST RIES
Grandma
Forgot
(and How I Found Them)

Nadine Aisha Jassat
Illustrated by Sandhya Prabhat

A NOTEBOOK FULL OF QUESTIONS

I AM

Today in English,
the teacher asked us to write
about who we are.

I could see my friend Jess
scribbling next to me,
her pen moving fast across the page.

I looked up at the prompt on the board,
the words 'I Am' standing out like a challenge,
like they're asking for something more
than I really understand.

I am   called Nyla Elachi.
       or NNN-EYYYE-LA to people I meet for the first time,
       or NYLA, NYLA, PANTS ON FIRE to a certain bully
       who I swear won't make me cry.
       I'm Sweetie to my grandma, and Sweet Pea to my mum.
       Both of them sound like: *mine*.

I am   a girl who helps look after her grandmother,
       and her memory-magic brain.
       My dad died when I was four.
       I don't know what he would have called me.
       Sweetie? Daughter? Nyla?

I am   the words 'It's going to be okay,'
       that I whisper to myself,
       whenever I feel afraid.
       I wear the same school jumper every day.
       It's way too big for me, but Mum says
       I've got to grow into its sleeves
       (even though they've already started to fray).

I am   the person who gets asked big questions,
       like *Where Are You From?* straight away,
       before someone has got to know me,
       their words trying to put me in a box, or a cage.

I am   the quiet voice that whispers,
       (even though I want to say: *None of your business*)
       after people have guessed a million countries
       that they think match my face:
       I'm mixed. My mum is white,
       and though people always think
       we don't look alike,
       I think it's because they're not looking right:
       they're not seeing what I see.
       My dad and grandma are from Zimbabwe,
       and their mix is Brown and Black,
       their mix is full of stories,
       stories that I wish I had,
       ever since my dad passed.
       Stories that are part of me.

I am   a girl who makes promises to everyone else,
       but if I was to make one to myself,
       it would be this:

       to have the words, one day,
       to say exactly what I mean.
       To know how to answer the question:
       'I Am'.

PART 1

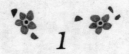

LIFE IS LIKE THE BUSES

MY MORNING

My morning started with the crunch of toast between teeth:
Mum + Grandma + Me.

It moved with our own flow:
Mum grabbed Grandma's red coat,
and I reminded Grandma how to put on her shoes,
as she leaned down and whispered:
'Time for dancing, Sweetie!'

'Hello, dear!' Grandma shout-waved
as she climbed into the day-care bus,
to a lady walking past.
'You're looking lovely today!'

Followed by the noise of a zip closing,
as Mum sneaked a note into my bag:

Have a
LOVELY DAY,
Sweet Pea.

And her stifled yawn,
after working back-to-back shifts,
in an office during the day,
and cleaning at night.
She's just one person trying to earn enough
to stretch over the three of us.

Then walking to school as fast as I can —
until I see a figure skulking towards me,
slowly filling me with dread:

'What're you looking at, Elachi?'

A BRIEF HISTORY OF HARRY

Harry is in the year above,
and for reasons
I can't understand,
he always seems to
single me
out
and make me
feel
on edge.
I've seen him do it to other people,
but not as much as me.

My friend Jess said,
that on a swimming trip in Juniors,
he stole someone's clothes,
and threw them in the pool.

Jess said that person now goes to another school.

I don't want that to happen to me.
I keep my head down,
hoping he'll leave me alone eventually —

but
        he never does.

WORDS IN THE MUD

When Harry's blue eyes look me up and down,
my reply falls out of my mouth,
and gets lost in the mud by my feet.

'Aren't you gonna answer me?
What. Are. You. Looking.
AT!'

Harry lunges,
his white hands spread out wide,
then laughs
as if he can see how
my tummy flips
uʍop ǝpısdn
and inside out,
as I start to feel smaller
and smaller
and less
and less like me,
until I see the smile up ahead of me
of the friendliest face
who pushes past Harry,
multicoloured bobbles bouncing in her light-brown hair,
linking her arm through mine:

'What's up, Elachi?'

'Hey, Jess.'

ALL ABOUT JESS

I've known Jess since first year,
when *everyone* was new to school,
but I was new to *here*.

The teacher asked us to introduce ourselves
to the person sitting next to us.
I didn't know what to say,
so, I tried: 'I've just moved from the other side of town.'

'Really?' Jess exclaimed enthusiastically,
freckles dancing across her cheeks.
'Tell. Me. *Everything*.'

Everything felt huge,
but I did my best:
I told her about me,
and Mum and Grandma.
After, she asked more and more:

'Would you rather own a chihuahua or a husky?'
'Are you a Gemini? Cancer? Libra? I KNEW IT!'
'We can have lunch together, if you want?'

That was over 365 lunches ago.
We've been friends ever since.

MISSING MARSHMALLOWS

It wasn't long before I opened up to Jess about Dad.

Lying on her bedroom floor,
doing homework for maths,
we were learning about fractions,
and had just been delivered hot chocolate by her dad,
with marshmallows balanced like fluffy clouds on top.

When I told her about my dad,
she listened.
'I wish I had more memories of him,' I said,
not adding how I wish
he would bring me hot chocolate
with his own custom topping,
or ask me about school.

Jess looked down at the checked lines
and scribbles on her workbook page.
'Maybe ... he's not gone completely,
in all the things that are left of him,'
she whispered,
before turning to me with the biggest smile,
'Like you! And you're super cool.'

If ¼ of a
marshmallow
is missing,
how much
is left?

And then we slurped our hot chocolates,
giggling as whipped cream tickled our noses.

If I'm what's left of Dad,
then Grandma is too —
she's his mum
(and my best friend).

What's left of him are the lines
around Mum's eyes and cheeks,
the ones from all the times he made her laugh
(and the ones from after he died).

And all of my questions,
that I wish I could ask him.
All the missing stories —
the sound of Mum's silence,
when I want to know more.

What's left of him are
Grandma's memories:
twinkling lights in the dark.
Memories which are
like shooting stars

slowly
fading
away.

ALZHEIMER'S (NOUN)

When Mum first told me
what Grandma's forgetting was called —
Alzheimer's —
I thought about how it sounded
like it had a
'*Hi*' in the middle
even though it feels like
the opposite, like
the person is slowly walking away.

Mum says to think of it like time-travel:
like Grandma's mind is journeying
to another time or place.
I see Grandma time-travel
when she calls me
                    Nurse?
                            Or   *Girl?*
                                    Or   *Honey?*
I try and remind her:
'Look, Grandma, it's me,
Sweetie!'

A name I love.
A name that feels so good to call my own.

But when she looks at me it's like
she's
                    not
        really
                    here.

When she looks at me
it's like she's living somewhere else,
and I'm the one far away,
reaching for those two letters:
'Hi'.
A word that I understand
in a bigger word that I really don't:
Alzheimer's.

FORM PERIOD

When Mr Davis calls my name,
I think about how it's the third time today
that I've heard 'Elachi',
but how each time it's felt different.

In Harry's mouth it feels hard,
like he's taken something precious to me,
and twisted it, tainted it.

In Jess's it feels like part of this whirlwind
of her, of all her different energetic words.
I know that if I looked in the Jess Dictionary,
Elachi would be listed under *friend*.

And from Mr Davis, it feels all 2D,
like it's missing its history,
its story.

STORIES LIKE ELACHI SEEDS

Recently, on a good day,
Grandma split open a cardamom pod,
and held it up to my nose.

'Elachi,' she said, pointing at the open line
running down the small seed pod.
'Elachi also means cardamom.'

We leaned down together,
and sniffed, the rich smell
filling our noses.

'Remember,' Grandma said,
and held me close.
'Elachi. It's my name.
The one I passed on to your dad,
and you. The one I'll never change.'

That's what my name means to me.
It means Grandma, and family.
It means stories, tucked up inside Grandma
like elachi seeds,
like the gold in a cardamom pod.

Happy
World Book Day!

When you've read this book, you can keep the fun going by swapping it, talking about it with a friend, or reading it again!

What do you want to read next? Whether it's **comics**, **audiobooks**, **recipe books** or **non-fiction** you can visit your school, local library or nearest bookshop for your next read – someone will always be happy to help.

SPONSORED BY

Changing lives through a love of books and reading.

World Book Day® is a charity sponsored by National Book Tokens